BHOOTA GAPPA

7 Short Horror Stories

PRATIKSHA MISRA

justutter

ISBN
Hardcase 979-8-89610-717-0
Paperback 979-8-89610-378-3

CONTENTS

INTRODUCING "BHOOTA GAPPA"

"It's dark and lonely,
then comes the fear,
that needs to show courage
of facing it before running away...
It's the scream that melts within your gut,
but unable to come out,
the resistance to encounter the world beyond...
allowing conversations with the spirits of the past
that have left you even though they
reside inside while struggling to hide..."

INTRODUCTION

"Bhoota Gappa", means "Ghost Stories", in the Odiya dialect, and that's my native language from the land of Lord Jagannath where I come from, called Odisha, an eastern state of India famous for its culture, food, handicraft and temples. This all started back in 1985, when we used to visit Buxibazar, Cuttack, our grandparents' home, during the summer holidays. As stories were a kid's portal to imagination back then, we were narrated an infinite number of stories by my grandmother (father's mom). Most of it in the genre of ghosts, spirits and black magic, which either she had experiences of her own or she narrated experiences of someone close to her from her childhood. She called it "Bhoota Gappa".

I name this book series in memory of my grandmother, who wanted to become a great educator some day and read a lot of books in various languages, despite being educated just till middle school.

Each book in this series consists of 7 short horror stories, followed by a snippet of a bigger horror story happening in parallel, with all the characters from these shorter stories. Some of these experiences are being shared for the first time and are stories inspired by an amalgamation of true stories and events. This will make your heart beats faster, your eyes get bigger and your mind a bit foggy, while you feel chillier as you walk deeper into the darkness of these haunting experiences. Hope you read it all and publish some honest feedback after you read.

* *All the stories and characters in this book are imaginary and were personal experiences shared by individuals. Any resemblance to anyone else's experiences or life events are purely coincidental.*

ACKNOWLEDGEMENT

For this set of stories, I thank my late grandmother, who contributed to most of the stories in this collection. My father, who himself is a writer, has shared with me numerous of his experiences, from his childhood to his adolescence. My friends, who have believed in me and have given me the opportunity to share their experiences in an anonymous manner. My mother, my maternal uncle, my brother, my husband, who have shared their unexplained experiences and continue to inspire me to write this portal of short horror stories, called "Bhoota Gappa".

AZAGKA: THE DAWN OF FEAR: THE BEGINNING

"Nobody knew

who her father was...

Nobody knew

What her father did...

Everyone knows her father got hungry

and devoured her mom...

But she doesn't believe it to be true.

Everyone sees her as a threat...

If only she knew that her father is

right where she thinks she is standing alone..."

The first time I tasted blood, I loved it. But my father did not want me to accept who I was. I loved women. I kept lying to everyone who I met, I kept denying that I was someone else. Until one day I met Shloka, a person who had no fear of accepting herself for who she was. She taught me everything that my father was not able to teach me. She and I became best of sisters in no time.

The first time I bled I felt sorry for myself, the stains all over my bathroom floor, the painful dilemma of shutting the door while hiding the pungent odor. But no one told me then, that blood discharge was power.

"There are vultures

out there,

to eat pieces of you,

while you don't

know, you have no clue,

I wish you knew...

But it's hard to say,

all everyone cares about

are tears, who cries

all day long,

but no one for,

if something's wrong,

without a drop of pity,

I want to say it,

I want to say it louder,

but they feel you are crazy,

as you are not going to

fall dead,

which means they,

still must live with you,

the vultures hunt in groups,

and one of them will

be nice to you.

They will listen at first,

as they have the deepest thirst,

they are going to slowly,

bleed you to death,

while the others watch

you die inside out..."

Pitch black vultures surrounding a carcass, flying, and jumping places, as they come closer to the corpse, and pull a piece of meat, from the dead, something red dangling on their beaks, while they chew them in.

I try to get closer to look at what they all are feeding on. When the anatomy of a body is out there, with the skin tattered to pieces, it's hard to focus on the face of a person.

Suddenly a vulture looks at me and comes running towards me with a pack of four following, I see a head ripped apart from the body at a distance and try to picture the little boy behind it. But with the vultures chasing me, I was starting to smell danger.

AzaGkA, means "Danger", and that's my name, and I am an orphan, who has the curse of seeing life beyond death. I stay with six of my siblings who are equally orphans. Twins, a sister and a brother; a sister who doesn't talk much or nothing at all; a brother who loves to hunt; a bossy elder sister who doesn't get along; and a little brother who can mimic anyone and everyone who he has ever met.

We stay with an old couple, who have been partners since forever, they are kind enough to keep us without question.

Now over to their stories and experiences, which will make you know them in a whole another dimension. Don't worry my story will be coming soon, so keep reading...

01

KILL: THAT WAS JUSTIFIED

*"Revenge is the courage
that overpowers
injustice"*

It was a little past midnight, and there was a power outage in Kandarpur, a small village in Derabish Tehsil in Kendrapara district of Odisha State, I had decided to sleep on the cot spread over my grandparents' terrace.

It was a moonlit night, with tall coconut trees looking down at me, while they tried to get my attention over the stars. The neighborhood had come to a standstill, with a constant hustle in the highway right next to the house, still ongoing but slightly lesser than usual.

Suddenly, I heard a distant jingle noise of bangles coming from a woman's hand, while walking.

I thought who at this mad hour is taking a stroll. The highway with a lot of trucks traveling all night long was right next to our entrance pavement and the other side of the road was quite blurry as sometimes the streetlights just didn't want to work.

Due to the power outage, it was very dark on both the housing areas of the road, but the light coming from the trucks and buses in the highway was the only way where I could see something visible and worth making sense of.

I got up and went to the edge of the terrace.

I could very vaguely identify a woman walking by and thought she is the one who must be wearing those bangles.

The next day I was woken up by a huge thud on the ground next to our terrace, it was a couple of ripe coconuts that fell off from the tree. I ran down to check with my grandmother and grandfather about last night.

While heading out the living room door, I met the helper – "Nanda Bhai" who used to come to my grandfather's ranch to milk the cows and help in delivering calves and preparing nutritious diet for the cows.

I asked him about last night and if he knew any lady or family who loves to take strolls past midnight.

He was unable to give me any sort of clarity, as he said he hardly is aware of knowing anyone in the neighborhood, who venture out that late, that too right next to the highway, which is quite dangerous to start off with.

Enquired the same with my grandmother, who was prepping her betel quid while sipping her morning tea, and she gave me a strange look, with one eyebrow raised as for a woman going on a walk at that hour of the night was a concerning news for her.

The next night, I thought of shouting out louder to warn the woman, of the atrocities she might face while walking beside a highway filled with heavy vehicles.

Just recently my grandfather was telling me the incident of how in the neighborhood a calf met with an accident on the highway. Calves when they are born tend to run a lot compared to a human baby, as they fumble and are unable to stand on their own, but still try their best to outrun the world behind them.

But she seemed to pay no heed to my words, and looked to be in hurry and her bangles jingle were rushed through.

"Fires have busted lanterns

and yet the broken glass pieces

have resisted melting away...

Fire has charred fingers

that still have pointed the wrong way

they have burned with smokes floating in air

they have learned to mix chokes with empty flare

If you happen to look at Fire, it has an empty stature...

but the flames rise to take the shape of a staunch posture...

Fire never speaks of the weak...

Fire just takes darkness to its peak...

In losses it reeks of the oblivion masses."

A pyre of holy fire, burning and I can see myself sitting in-front of it and pouring oil, as the flame rises and touches the sky with black smoke. I could see someone beyond the darkness, I leave the pyre and go behind chasing them. But unfortunately find myself in the middle of a dark forest with the holy fire being far away from my reach. I get pushed by a pair of hands, and I start falling, I want to get up, but I am unable to. Can someone wake me up, can I shout?

I opened my eyes, sweating all over. I got up and went down the staircase to grab some water. Everyone in the house was asleep. It was around 4:00 am on the clock.

This was the second night with no power in the village, but frankly speaking with the cool breeze blowing, no one needed an air conditioner as we were sleeping, eating, and living just fine. Let me immerse you through the experience that I have lived to remember through the rest of my life. The summer holidays, where we used to come to the paradise build by my late grandparents (Ajja & Aaee in Odiya)

The Story of An Untold Paradise: Kandarpur (my grandparents' abode)

The picture of a tall sturdy body, a straight cut face, covered up with broad brown specs usually hiding the wide eager eyes behind it...

Leaning by the side of the tall white gate...since dawn peeking now and then, so that he doesn't miss out the moment...

The White Gate

Quality - Helped us swinging ourselves from one side of the end to the other.

Quantity - More than one kid at a time.

Special Factor - Made us believe all of us had the mighty talent to become Spider-Man one day.

His face used to brighten up at the sight of our incoming auto-rickshaw, when slowly it trudged down the hill, where his amazingly beautiful ranch was situated...surrounded by tall coconut trees, a huge pond, a cow shelter, heaps of hay, a highly nutritious kitchen garden, acres of farm lands where you can just run all day long...will get into deep analysis as I go further....

*The land of my Ajja (Maternal Grandfather) and Aaee (Maternal Grandmother), **"Kandarpur",** The Paradise, which I would be talking about was called **"BHAWANI-BHAWAN".** My Ajja named it in the loving name of his lovely wife, my Aaee "Bhawani".*

The ranch was situated just by the highway, an uphill raw road from the ranch made its way to the highway. The uphill road was surrounded by tall coconut and date trees on one side and the other side was a small pond where wild flowers sometimes made a magnetizing sight to look at.

I will come back to it later, first let me complete our pompous arrival to "BHAWANI-BHAWAN". The auto- rickshaw usually agreed to come down the hill even though our baggage was quite heavy for the 15-day long summer vacations. Ajja, excited since morning used to grab the bags and call out for his son's to help him out...Munnu...(Munna- The name of his youngest son, whom he used to call Munnu) and Babu...

(The name of his eldest son, younger to two of his sisters, my mother and her sister

*Meanwhile, Mom used to bow down and take her dearest father's blessings, tears rolled down my mom's eyes when she touched her father's feet with gratitude, which she used to wipe it off as soon as possible, but I always caught a glimpse of it. Happiness is all over the place while a daughter visits her home after she is married off. My Mom is the eldest of all her 4 siblings, with 2 sisters and 2 brothers. Being the eldest, she was the favorite of her father, he called her **"The Engine"**, to which all the rest of the bogies followed in the track of life....*

My brother and I rush inside after taking our Ajja's and Mamu's (Uncle- Mom's brother) blessings, to meet our beautiful and charming Aaee. My mother comes along with her dad and brothers talking to each other. Though I was a kid, I remember Ajka always asking mom "Maa tu theek achu???" (My dear daughter hope you are doing well in your life)...

The ranch covered a large area, so the house, "Bhawani Bhawan" had 2 entrance doors, one for the guests and one for us. We used to rush through the surrounding garden, the cow shelter, the huge pond and many trees to get into the second door. Just adjacent to the pond, was the door on a high cemented altitude having a bench with Ajja's walking stick kept beside the door and we can see the vast kitchen garden attached to it. Attached to the kitchen garden was a small tin door which was the entrance to the endless farm plots.

The moment we entered the door, our eyes would be glittering with happiness. I don't have any specific reason for that ambrosial feeling. Rushing inside...a strong aroma from the tea boiling in the tea kettle...

Aaee had a routine to sleep till 10 'o' clock, but the day we reached we used to bug her and at times even she used to wake up looking at her tiny tots...and her daughter.

Back to that night....

Suddenly I heard a sudden screech triggered by a brake taken by a truck driver on the highway after which I could hear people from adjacent houses gathering up in their patio.

I quickly rushed downstairs and woke up my grandfather, and he accompanied me through the entrance gate.

There was a huge crowd stalled at the highway, and as we went closer, we could see a dead body filled with blood and a crushed head, I turned around as I couldn't bear the sight and instantly my eyes fell on some red bangles scattered all over that spot.

At first, I thought it was the woman, who got killed, and felt guilty as I should have said something. Later I got to know that apparently there was an incident of a newlywed woman who got killed by her husband and in-laws by being pushed out of a moving vehicle, and now it was her husband who was lying dead at the same spot.

No one knew what he was doing here at this hour, that part was still unexplained, but after that night I did not get to see the woman nor hear bangles jingling past midnight anymore.

Luckily after that incident, the next day the power was back on, and it was good to stay indoors, watching back-to-back cartoon series after 3 long days.

I preferred to sleep indoors until the end of my summer holidays that year.

"In Dussehra Lord Ram killed his own inner demons depicted in the form of Ravana's 10 heads, which were jealousy, pretenses, anger, temptations, revenge, arrogance, wickedness, restlessness, dubiousness, and bitterness.

That made him win against all odds resulting in a supreme force to light the pathways for the ones that had been yearning to go home uniting him with his family. So, let's kill our inner demons and spread the light yet again amongst folks who have caught up in a storm of misfortune cause kindness is life changing..."

But I am sure if revenge is not kept in order, the soul of even the kindest being can go through major discomfort. After a couple of years, I lost it all and was thrown to the dungeons of darkness amongst 7 others, fighting the same battle of loneliness.

That was the story of **Shloka**, my sister who doesn't talk much. As she lost her voice, in an accident that changed her whole life.

* * * * *

02

SHADOW: SOMEONE'S FOLLOWING

"I release my yesterdays to scintillating shadow that reflects
a mirage of emotions,
from which I learn to stay
away from while carving a realistic tomorrow..."

This is the story of my youngest brother **Viansh**.

I had the funniest childhood, born to someone, who didn't want that I should know them at all. Discarded outside a temple, the people around started to call me "Viansh", that meant part of God.

Until one day, my spiritual father decided to get rid of me, by donating me to an orphanage. I never thought being in an orphanage was going to be such a heavenly experience, alongside 6 other siblings and a loving father and a charming mother. I was reborn on the very same day and couldn't be more thankful to the one who made this possible. Somehow, that day I felt like a part of me just had to spiritually connected to him in some way for this miracle that pulled me in as a family.

But since childhood, I had a weird problem of being bothered by nightmares, quite realistic and dramatic. I would be pulled into battles, pushed through tall buildings, left to burn on pyre, or chased by wild animals. I had woken up to find myself heavily bruised some days but haven't given that much of a thought as I know for sure, I can't be killed in my sleep.

I will share one such dream with you...

It was around 9:30-10pm, I was heading back from my friend's place. I had preferred to walk that day, as my cycle was in the repair shop. Just then I sensed someone walking right behind me.

Sometimes when you walk at night, where the streetlights aren't cooperating, you end up getting startled by your own shadow. So, at first, I felt like the same thing was happening to me, where I was misinterpreting my own shadow.

But soon I realized that wasn't the case. It seemed to be something real. The road suddenly got dark; my heart had started to thump faster. The moon wasn't clear that night, and it was starting to get absolute dark suddenly.

"What is it?"

"Who is this following at this hour?"

"Why is that person not talking?"

It was getting harder to breathe. My armpits were filled with sweat, and both of my ears were unusually warm.

I could somehow now feel it closer, right behind, smelling my hair. I was getting numb, speechless, stopping my every movement, to cease existence. I had absolutely no courage to look around.

Finally, I turned into a street, where there were some streetlights blinking vigorously. Something inside me pushed me to give up the nervous act and show some valor. I turned back, and as soon as I did that, a shadow flew right across the street and stuck to the branch of a tall banyan tree.

While I looked at it, it was a strange sight as it looked like a bat with legs dangling upside down. I didn't have the courage to verify what I was seeing, but it very much looked like a person, staring back at me with bloodshot eyes.

I didn't give it another thought and started running, as fast as I could, and for a while, it seemed as if it was running behind me. But I lost its trail when I reached home. I opened my eyes, and it was daybreak, but for some reason I saw sweat stains all over my bed sheet and pillow covers.

"I hear a howl

Look out of the window

Find a shadow that calls

Closed my eyes shut

Stay steady

Breathing heavy...

Trying to flee while the howling haunts

Gathered courage

Starting to walk into the dark

Where all things except you talk

It's like the trees are staring down

And the roads push you backwards

So, no matter how much forward you go

You find yourself back at the same place

Am I even walking right?

Your heart beats louder than the noiseless night

Some car screeches at the background

Echoing through the vacuum

Is someone hurt?

There are looks in the dark

That only books have spoken about

There are looks behind you

That only sniffing can rat you out

The thought of being followed

The thought of seeing the shadow of someone

you don't want to...

Keep looking

Don't be afraid

Says the mind

While your heart keeps saying

Go home, and stay blind throughout the rest of the night..

Speak to no one until asked

Coz weak is never alone to be tasked

The door closes on you

Wondering why it chose to do so

The logic is off

▶ Pratiksha Misra ◀

As a black creature whiffs off

Right next to you

Perhaps I am getting tired

Well, that's a lie

Although it sounds comforting

Wind whispers

There's nothing you can do

What happens in the dark

Isn't for humans to embark

The evil spirit has risen

While houses are locked

Haunting the woods

They scatter their wicked locks

So even if they knock

Don't you open.

Or you will gawk at them

While they mock

Blood thirst

Is the curse they take with them

While drinking blood

Isn't the thinking kind

We all do it

But never say

Only to blame the monsters

To be insane

Each one of us

Sleep in pain

Falling apart in dreams

To get up for the day

That seems like

Somethings did go away at night

To be hidden between

The worlds

Where we all believe to

Belong to a different dimension."

* * * * *

03

I HEARD SCREAMS: A HIDDEN WARRIOR

"Everyone was quiet...

One was shattered.

No one earns it right.

Faith was scattered.

Words were over-polite...

One had scars.

It started to pour in slight.

My eyes had drops tonight.

White came down...

Flowers for the crown.

Gathered every courage...

To meet the verbiage.

Hearts swelled with each other.

But never got further.

They would rather die...

But lie to each other.

Though white in color...

They were always painted.

Though pure in valor.

They were portrayed as tainted.
Now the crowd doesn't fight...
As one has lost her very right.
From her bag wide open...
She showers the painted flowers.
That gets washed off by rain..."

I lived in Malad (West) in Mumbai back then. I had a family, everything was, let's just say, better than perfect. We were like painted flowers, no matter what the mood of the hour, our family was picture perfect. Until a bomb-blast happened and my life was shattered.

The best part of living in Mumbai is life moves on, no one deliberately attempts to remind you off the lost. No one asks you for the time, everyone asks you for direction as they know that time is running at a faster pace and no matter how much we try, we cannot outrun it.

I was brought to an orphanage, and life had to go on. I had to get a job, get some income, and earn enough to be able to get back the picture-perfect life that was stolen from me. The Six other kids look needy to me, for me this is just a stop gap solution.

However, after the demise of my parents, I started getting nightmares, every night sharp at 2-3am, waking up whoever was accompanying me to bed that night or sometimes the whole family of Nine.

It is as if my dead parents wanted to visit me, but during their visit, there were many others on the way, who would make the journey unbearable and nerve wrecking. Every night I would wake up and cry painfully for about 30 minutes, as Viansh would mimic me every day at the breakfast table.

I would usually forget all the nightmares in the morning, but some of the nightmares would leave a scar on me for a long period of time. Sometimes I would see them dying and burning into pieces, sometimes I would see them crying back at me, asking me to save them. Sometimes it would be a dark cave of shadows, surrounding me by forming a circle of darkness, sometimes it would be just me being killed by my own parents.

I had a sense, darkness was like a friend to me, lurking around, sitting besides, knocking at the window of a moving bus, staring at me from the bushes in the backyard. But with each passing time, I had managed to befriend it and was getting less bothered by its presence.

"It's dark and lonely,

Then comes the fear,

That needs to show courage

Of facing it before running away...

It's the scream that melts within your gut,

But unable to come out,

The resistance to encounter the world

beyond...

Allowing conversations with the spirit

that have left you even though they

reside inside while struggling to hide..."

I rushed to the train station to catch the last local back to my place at 2:00 AM, as a meeting with a customer had extended. The train was mostly empty, with a few passengers like me heading back from late-night shifts. One of the best things about Mumbai is that you're rarely alone. I exited at my station and planned to walk home, as my apartment was only a 15–20-minute walk away.

The station was nearly deserted at this hour. As I stepped outside, I heard a distant scream that startled me. It sounded like multiple women screaming at once. I gathered my courage and continued walking slowly.

Every day at the station, I met my transgender friend, Radha. She had helped me during Mumbai's rains, power outages, and even when I lost my parents to the blasts. This had created a strong bond between us. She always greeted me with a warm smile, and no matter how late I was for work, I would give her a 10-rupee note and wish her a good day. In return, she would bless me wholeheartedly, as if she understood the struggles I had faced in this new chapter of my life.

Back to that dreadful night, I could faintly see a group of women sitting in a circle in the middle of the road. There was no light in that area, and I had to cross under the bridge. At first, I hesitated, as something felt wrong. It was a moonless night (Amavasya), and I hadn't realized it until then. I saw the group eating something, and suddenly heard footsteps behind me, as if someone was following. Just then, I saw a tiny, frail woman walking while still seated. She noticed me, and then came the chaotic, shrill screams that deafened my ears. I began to tremble, and sweat was dripping from all parts of my body.

What were these women eating at this hour in the corner of the road? Just then, I saw a woman wearing a red saree running towards them, shouting. I closed my eyes, expecting her to be attacked, but instead, I saw them all flying away like a flock of crows, cawing through the sky.

"Wait! Was that, Radha?"

She was coming towards me, her hands held mine tightly. She walked me home without saying a word. I thanked her profusely. She folded her hands and said that those were evil spirits were devouring a dead dog. Because she is a devotee of Maa Kali (Goddess of Evil), they ran away. She advised me to consider moving back to the orphanage to be safer with the rest.

This was the story of **Abhaya,** one of my sisters, who always wants to run away from us but the darkness within her doesn't free her, no matter how hard she tries. We all try to keep her happy as always.

04

THE OLD SCHOOL HALLWAY: COURAGEOUS STATURE

"Take a quick whiff by the edge of the grass.

Sneaking in a couple dew drops.

Just as clear as glass.

Into your palm.

That looks like a charm.

You have all for yourself.

Playing a riff while gazing the clouds.

Finding the dollop...

From a selective crowd.

Galloping adrift the caricature...

That stands stiff is none other than your stature."

This is a story of a brave heart my brother, **"Ekaksh"**, who never knows when to give up.

Growing up in an orphanage, I had never imagined having my own biological family. When I was adopted, tears welled up in my eyes. Meeting my new family, I knew I had found the loving home I'd always longed for.

I have been a sick child for quite some time now, I am either all day in bed crying in pain or watching outside the window, to see how free the birds are. I was an orphan, with no knowledge of what made me come to this world and frankly speaking maybe some part of myself never wanted to know, as to why?

We were forced to go to a catholic school, which was literally surrounded by graveyard all over the place. There were all sorts of stories about how at night people encountered shadows while walking past the walls of the school.

It was science project season, and I was working on an experiment in the lab, just then I got a tingling effect inside my stomach, and I rushed to the bathroom. As usual, in a school of mischievous members, someone thought of locking me out. I had soon passed out, after vomiting the bad curry we had for breakfast that day. When my eyes opened, it was already dark outside, I was nervous, as I was trying to shout out loud at the same time I was crying perpetually. I very well knew that no one was around to help. Just then I heard footsteps in the corridor.

"Is there someone here?", called out the heavy voice.

I was in tears, but at the same time happy to know that there was help. I replied as loud as possible, and then he opened the door. He was a tall figure, with loads of beard and had a very kind sense of humor. He asked me about my backpack and walked me outside the school premises to the orphanage that was just two miles from the school.

He asked me which grade I was, he said he used to teach math to high school and had a habit of always checking test papers at night. He dropped me at the gate, and I rushed in to make sure dinner was still available as I was starving. Then I went back to thank him, but he wasn't around. Surprisingly, a black cat came closer to me and rubbed its head on my knee and ran away.

The next day when I inquired about the teacher, he was nowhere to be found. I didn't give up and decided to go to the archive room to check all the class pictures to find him out, suddenly I found him smiling alongside 8th graders for the year 1989, and this was 1994. I rushed to ask the caretaker of the archive room about his whereabouts. When the caretaker heard this story, his eyes went wider, and he checked with me repeatedly. Then he took me to what I initially thought to be the principal's office. He took me instead to the student counselor. I was worried about what was going on.

The counselor gave me some cookies and milk and showed me a picture of that man. She said that the person who helped me the night before was her father, and she was glad that I got to meet him. However, she said, with tears in her eyes, that he was no more since the past 5 years, as he committed suicide in that very bathroom where I got locked the night before. "But I have heard from a lot of students that he does come and strolls the old school hallway, at times when no one is around either by taking the form of a cat or sometimes is his original form", said the counsellor.

After that day, I recovered for good, and for some reason, became a hero that ruled the math world, even aced my board exams, I still feel meeting him had something to do with the miracle.

* * * * *

05

A LADY IN WHITE

Now begins the story of my twin brother and sister. Their names are **"Arit"**, meaning "worthy of praise" and **"Asmi"**, meaning "I am". Both lost their entire family during the war between two religious cults, and finally decided to be away from any beliefs that devour the sense of humanity.

Once upon a time, they had everything they had wished for; a huge family of uncles, aunts, grandparents, cousins, distant relatives and a huge house, filled with great values of togetherness. Until one day, everything was lost by the death of one of their favorite cousins, who lost faith in life.

After which there were a sequence of untimely death and remorse, which was struck endlessly making their legacy take the plight of trauma and solitude.

As a result of this immense loss, both Arit and Asmi had become ruthless and fearless in their life. Neither did they fear the living nor the dead. Arit would be a nightwalker, with mostly sleeping in graveyards, or marching through dense forests, finding answers for people who seek darkness within. Asmi, would accompany him, or sometimes, be making potions, experimenting solutions, in her lab in the basement, filled with old books, dead or living animals in cages, plants, herbs of all kinds. Let's just stay, nothing can scare them anymore as their instincts remain hard core.

"Death is the birth of your value."

Sweating the last drop..

He drags himself..

To the corner of the shelf.

Heart beats faster..

Getting short of breath.

He has to fight death..

Unknowingly alive.

After a deep dark dive.

The room getting darker..

But that doesn't scare the lurker.

If there isn't a tall shadow.

On the wall that swallows.

Making it hard to see.

Making it harder to break free.

His bruised knee.

Urging to flee.

As his body trembles.

Tightening the shake within.

Finding a way to a never-ending win.

There lies the key...

Opening to the vast sea.

Emptiness wallows.

Shouting gets unheard

Until ears ask him to stop being absurd.

There's a leap.

That gets steep.

A final weep.

With sunset running away..

The moon shines..

Glistening his cry for a while..

With a sudden stop..

Fear ceases.

His breathing eases.

Lot of stories from their childhood memoir, here is one which Arit and Asmi had narrated to me when we first met.

"Arit, it's getting late for breakfast, where are you!", I heard my mother, but was not willing to let go of the newly found magazines in the storeroom. This room was one of my favorites in my grandpa's place, full of old items, games, puzzles, magazines. I was always sure of finding something which would make the rest of my summer holidays interesting. Social Reform Society, Buxibazar, Cuttack, and my "Bapa's" place (I used to call my grandpa as "Bapa" and my grandmother as "Maa") was where me, my mother and my sister had to spend at least 30 days of the 45 days long summer holidays every year.

Being extremely optimistic by nature, I successfully made the Social Reform society a playground.

It's a big area to start with; the office and the house of the President are adjacent to each other, so you can always look out for space in Bappa's office if you are bored of the house. There was sprawling greenery surrounding the establishment with coconut trees and a pond in the back yard. This pond seldom had fish unlike the one at my Ajja's residence. I tried fishing unsuccessfully once or twice. There were some mango trees, jackfruit and banana adjacent to the walls fencing the backyard and rubbing shoulders with those of the Swaraj Editor's Office, who happened to be our neighbor.

The garden in front of our house and the office had a variety of flowers and fauna. There was a red colored bench in front of the office which was once covered by an umbrella of the "Tagar Phoola Gaccha" (a white flower tree). I and my sister used to do a lot of running around there, climbing the tree, jumping around, sucking nectar, chewing flower buds, making sword sticks, throughout the day.

We had the servant's quarter where the workers / attendants who were generally employed by "Baapa" used to stay. It was also a part of my adventure to explore their quarters, make friends with their children, exchange goodies, and include their assistance in my day-to-day activities, plans and games. Two of them that I very well remember were "Rama" and "Gholaka". There was a rickshaw parked just outside the house which was always at the disposal of "Bappa" and "Maa". The rickshaw driver used to report every evening. I usually was called upon by "Baapa" to assist him in his daily evening rounds. The only attractions of these rounds were the deer park and the colorful fountains in Tulsipur those days (these are no longer operational).

The library of the society's office was well stocked with good books. Most of these books were purchased by "Bappa" on his trips to the USA and Europe. He also happened to be associated with various programs of the United Nations, in what capacity was completely unknown to me at that time. In those times such books like the "Britannica Encyclopedia" were rare, hard to procure and extremely expensive. "Bapa" always ensured that every book that we picked up from the library was well accounted for and returned in time. Reading those books as a kid was a priceless experience for me.......

I and Asmi would spend days exploring the vast grounds of our grandparents' house. I was the leader, and she, the eager follower. Like many young sisters, she often tried to emulate me, adopting a more boyish demeanor. My guidance and friendship have been invaluable, as she continues to look up to me without regret.

The adults who worked at the nearby office adored us. Even the kitchen staff and cleaners became our friends, adding a touch of excitement to their daily routines. We played with them, listened to their adventurous tales (some embellished, I'm sure), and found solace in their company. In the absence of other children or modern entertainment, they were our saviors on this lonely island.

Asmi always had a fondness for animals. The vast grounds provided ample opportunities to interact with stray puppies, kittens, and even a frisky calf. However, my mother was strict about bringing animals home, so she had to keep her interactions secret.

One day, she brought home a kitten, which she cherished dearly. But I being a mischievous brother, along with my friends, decided to play a prank on her. We threatened to kill the kitten using electric shocks, terrifying her and making her believe that we had already done it.

She was heartbroken and wanted to retaliate. However, when the next day, she found the kitten roaming around, she got scared that she had seen the spirit of a dead cat, which made her not leave her room for a while.

The house was surrounded by a large garden with various trees. The office was adjacent to our living quarters. My grandparents occupied a room partially connected to the office. Beyond that was a long corridor leading to the dining hall, which had a pavement on one side and a cowshed on the other. The pavement served as a path to the outdoor toilet, a common feature in older houses. The path was lined with greenery, and at the end was a pond.

To discourage us from wandering around the house, Granny used to tell us ghost stories about the place. These tales sent shivers down my spine, but Asmi became more intrigued, turning into a miniature Sherlock Holmes, eager to solve the mysteries around him.

This is one of Asmi & Arit's Experience ...

It was a pitch-black night, and we were alone at our grandparents' house. The old-fashioned bathroom was located at the far end of the backyard, a five-to-ten-minute walk down a long, dimly lit courtyard lined with bushes and a swampy pond. Even during the day, people avoided the pond, so going there at night was unthinkable.

My brother urgently needed to use the bathroom, but I had avoided it in the nights for the entire two weeks of our visit, unless someone accompanied me and constantly communicated while I was inside. The flickering lights, the howling street dogs, and the eerie silence made the situation even more unsettling. I stood guard outside, armed with a torchlight, as I watched my brother enter the bathroom.

Suddenly, something caught my eye. A white object seemed to be floating above my head. As I looked up, I saw a woman in white, gliding along the electric wires that stretched over the walls to the neighbors. The dim light made it difficult to discern details. I shivered and began to sweat as the woman vanished into thin air, followed by a chilling cat's cry.

A moment later, I saw something white falling into the pond. To my horror, a figure emerged from the water, resembling a cat but wearing a brown sack. The shadow it cast as it walked was that of a woman.

My brother and I watched this spectacle in terror, then rushed inside and bolted the door. We ran to the caretaker's house next door, seeking comfort. Seeing us in such a state, they offered us water and tried to calm us down.

The next day, workers hired by my grandparents recovered a skeleton from the pond, hidden in a brown sack. The workers discarded the skeleton and used some iron nails to seal the pond, from evil spirit, they even called an "Aghori Baba"*, who chanted some hymns to lockdown the spirit in the pond.

After we returned from our holidays, granny used to still complain about the lady in white, and used to tell us about few incidents, where she has seen that woman couple of times, in the backyard window. The workers in the house had stopped, venturing out late in the evening, especially close to the pond.

*Aghori baba are a sect of people, who dwell in cremation grounds, smearing ashes on their bodies, using human skulls as utensils and eating flesh from human corpses. They are known to have a connection with evil spirits.

* * * * *

06

ROOM: LUCKY ESCAPE

We live with a couple, who have lost everything, but they don't mind looking at the brighter side of it all. They are our dads, **Ram** and **Daksh**, who live with us in the same house and have given all 7 of us new lives alongside their own.

This is the story of Ram.

"Behind Dusk..

is a rusted window,

that looks at every shadow,

like a broken piece,

of its own..

While giving shape

to someone's darkness,

letting out their hope,

that light is close by.."

As a bachelor, I found this surprisingly affordable one-bedroom apartment, which was hard to resist given my recent job and limited budget. Unfortunately, my early morning shift hours forced me to adjust to a new sleep schedule. Before my alarm could go off, I was startled by the sound of a nearby door opening.

This was strange because the landlord had assured me that the adjacent rooms were empty and there wouldn't be any noise issues.

Within seconds, I heard another door creaking open and the sound of footsteps, but there were no voices. It seemed like people were entering their rooms at this unusual hour, but they were neither talking nor turning on lights. It was a moonless night, and even the streetlights were out. Something was amiss. As I wandered around, my heart pounded when a shadow appeared beside my door, ready to enter. I tried to grab a broken broom from the closet, but my door was already wide open, and there was no one there.

I rushed outside and shouted, "Who's there?" My voice echoed back, and a cold shiver ran down my spine. I started sweating profusely. Later that day, I learned from my neighbor that the room I had been staying in had a history of unexplained deaths in the past few years. This discovery prompted me to leave the apartment and move to a hostel with roommates.

* * * * *

07

HANDS: LOST LOVE

"We all

are trapped

in our own

prison

of emotions,

that don't

accept us,

don't

tell us,

don't pull us

out.

But the moment

we make our

minds

to break free,

they push us

deep down,

into an

indefinite

frown,

showcasing

a memory mirage

that pierce

like the thorny

crown of

where will

you go from there..."

I had been by her side throughout our lives. Now, as a husband in a wheelchair, I could do little more than watch as she faded away. It was a dark, stormy night, and the rain had been falling since morning. It was past 11:00 PM, and we had finished dinner hours ago. Tiksha had been bedridden for over a month, her voice and memory fading. I would read to her, turn off the lights, and retire to my room.

That night, I had a strange feeling that this was it. She closed her eyes, and I knew she was leaving me forever. A power outage plunged the house into darkness. Alone, I cried and called out her name. Helpless, I waited for the morning, with death at my side.

As I wept uncontrollably, I felt a gentle touch on my shoulders. It was eerily familiar, like the comforting touch of her hands when I was frustrated. Fear gripped me, and I searched for a candle or torch. To my astonishment, my wheelchair began to move, guiding me to light a candle. "Daksh, why are you sitting in the dark?", said Tiksha. I scanned the room, but there was no one there except my deceased wife in the next room. For a moment, I hoped she had somehow come back to life.

The next morning, I had dozed off, and neighbors began to arrive after the storm. I noticed something on her hands: the threads from my shawl, which I had been wearing in my wheelchair. In that moment, I knew she had been with me all night, even after she had passed away.

* * * * *

IT'S NOT MY STORY, YET!

It starts with me going and visiting a house, of my past. I never knew it was my past, I never knew I had a past that dwelled in this house, until I found myself confronting myself but unable to help myself out of the darkness.

We were off to one of our richest cousin's wedding in Assam, and for the first time going to live in a house, which was larger than all of our collective houses and apartments put together. All of us were extremely excited and the wedding was being planned in a royal manner with event planning, rehearsal dinners, shopping, late night parties, everything one can dream of. Suddenly one night, while taking a call on the terrace, I could notice a small girl, between seven to nine years old, sitting on a bench behind the building, all by herself. When I called back at her, she looked at me, her face dark but with sorrowful eyes holding her arms up, gesturing to me to come, but when I went downstairs the back door was locked.

I kept getting up the entire night, thirsty, feeling miserable but her face seemed very familiar to me. The next day I asked around, but the staff gave me a worried look and requested me to avoid going to the terrace or the backside of the building at night. There was the "Mehendi" event, and I had caught a stomach bug, so I was sitting in the corridor, near the bathroom. The lights suddenly flickered, after which I could see the same little girl from far, running from something and getting up the stairs to the terrace. I followed her, and then suddenly the terrace door closed behind me, and the little girl was nowhere.

I heard a loud scream and rushed to see who was at the back of the building. I found a man doing something to that girl and running away. I rushed downstairs but the doors were locked to go to the back of the building.

But the next day no one was talking about any accidents. I kept sweating, not feeling well and was starting to come down with something, when an old lady in a wheelchair looked at me and asked me to sit closer to her. She said I looked very similar to a little girl, who used to be her friend and lived here a long time back. Unfortunately, she was killed in a gruesome incident and her parents sold the property after that.

When I saw her picture, I couldn't imagine as I was basically that same girl in my childhood days, but probably in very different times as she had been dead for over 80 years now. The woman told me that I must leave the place sooner.

This is **Avyanna's** *Story.*

"If the night is alone,

it will choose to stay on its own

without coming to my place or yours.

If the night had a tone,

it will choose to talk to its inner self

without trying to convince me or yourself,

or chasing the annoying little elf

back into the dense dark forest.

If the night could love,

it will always pick the moon

as it changes the skin of even an evil goon,

I cannot wait until I found all about it

that's gone too soon...."

My Story Begins...

* * * * *

AZAGKA: THE DAWN OF FEAR: THE BEGINNING

The Final Curse Hour

The world was fading around me. Dirt clung to my battered body, blood seeping from every wound. Knees, arms, face - all a testament to the brutal fight. My mind raced, searching for a flicker of hope.

Viansh, Shloka—lifeless beside me. *"Are they dead?"*

A scream pierced the chaos, Ekaksh's desperate plea for my survival. Near the pyre, Arit and Asmi, their frantic movements cast long, eerie shadows. A green potion, poured into the smoldering flames, accompanied by a haunting chant. Death's icy grip tightened around me, but I clung to the faintest glimmer of life, a defiant whisper against the encroaching darkness."

"Where is Abhaya?"

"What happened here?"

"Did I break the curse after all?"

"Did I meet him?"

There are four worlds existing in parallel. One is the world we live in; the second one is the world we come from; third one is the world where spirits keep dwelling for their loved ones; and fourth one is the world where evil tries to overpower the land of dead.

Introducing AzaGka's World by Ashvath (her father)

Meet AzaGka, a 42-year-old woman, who navigates the treacherous divide between academia and the dark world. By day, she dissects timeless texts, a respected English Literature professor. However, as the night falls, she sheds her scholarly guise, transforming into a relentless investigator, her heart steeped in the shadows of "Shikaar Nagar" - A place where ordinary lives are swallowed whole, a realm where survival hinges on a bloodline steeped in darkness.

AzaGka, a lone warrior amidst a pack of predators, her existence a precarious dance between the light of knowledge and the devouring depths of the unknown."

Her orphanage supports a community well versed with not just evil forces but resolving unchartered territories, of workforce beyond death. Her mission is to search for the missing ones, the left-out ones, the unexplained deaths, unexplained murders, strange occurrences in local areas, dark magic practices that were harming the locals, the practice of witchcraft, unethical supernatural powers.

"Shikaar Nagar" was well known for unidentified attacks. This is the place AzaGka was born, and she had lost everyone in this place, including her father. Surrounded by dense forest and wild animals, in a large patch of land, most of the civilization was built on top of a graveyard property.

Ekaksh, her elder brother a brave man, is a 45-year-old cop, serving the local police association, for over 20 years now. **Arit and Asmi** are dark sorcerers, **Shloka** their apprentice. While **Abhaya,** even though she tries to stay away from all this, her past pulls her into the debacle of being omnipotent. **Viansh** is still finishing high school, but very much a yes sayer, always with AzaGka wherever she goes.

Her past haunts her present, while her father, that's me, always remains alongside her to resolve any foul play, encountered during AzaGka's investigation. I visit her from the spirit world, as the land of living isn't where I belong anymore.

I can read minds...

As AzaGka Says, "I cannot see him but feel him, and the day I will finally be able to see him, I will free him from me completely. That's the reason I avoid following him through."

Ram and Dev are gay partners, my childhood friends and descendants of the "Tamas Gotra" – followers of a dark cult". Two of them are brave dark warriors, who come from the world of dark arts but try to be away from it as much as possible. They don't actively embark on taking part in AzaGka's quests, but they don't stop her either. AzaGka, Abhaya, Asmi, Arit, Ekaksh, Shloka and Viansh are ever thankful to them for having given them an opportunity to have a family each of them so longed for. As all of them couldn't have survived this realm all by themselves, after the tragic losses that each of them has endured in their lives.

Now over to AzaGka and her story

Current Hour

A tiger running and clutching my face in between its paws, while I struggled to get out.

"Are you fine, AzaGka?", asked Viansh, as I had started to choke in my sleep.

I woke up, and rushed to the bathroom, I was late!

I have had this dream of this same tiger for quite some time now. It's as though, it's trying to tell me something.

Everyone was seated at the table, having breakfast, our morning ritual.

I took the burnt toast, and kissed Ram on the forehead, I kept thinking what could the nightmare mean? I realized to have forgotten my glasses without which I become a next-door neighbor to blindness. Sometimes I believe every disability has to do something with your brain as it's definitely linked with what you think, you start believing it, as to what you really are.

Just last week I had forgotten it twice but survived except few incidents here and there which followed in the chronological order:

- Spilled ink all over Mr. Mathur's thesis.
- 10 heavy collisions with every single person who confronted me in the corridor, including Mr. Mathur again.
- And just read "making out" loud in front of the class filled with 50 teenagers out of which one of them

corrected me with a sheepish smile, that the word was "melting out", which was written by none other than me on the black board just a few minutes back.

I opened the garage door, and started my sea green scooter, it was my dad's. Just then a car met my scooter at the intersection, honking as loudly as possible.

After which I saw a little girl in yellow shorts and a t-shirt with classification of multiple puppy types, running towards me. I tried to use my brakes, but she had already fainted. I got off and rushed inside to get her a glass of water. She was gone. I did have an intuition that I had seen that t-shirt somewhere.

When I took a closer look at our entrance footpath it read, "you are cursed".

I needed to rush for my class, so I ignored the dialect of the threat and drove past it. After which a series of back-to-back events occurred.

I went back to being a small girl.

I had a mom who used to work as a farmer.

The village had a strong presence of a man eater.

"Are you okay miss?", enquired one of my students.

Ohh Boy!!

I had written gibberish on the board, instead of Hamlet's monologue highlights. Just then I saw my brother Viansh was staring outside from the window. I rearranged my schedule and rushed outside.

"What Happened?", I asked.

He whispered, "There is a man eater on the prowl, it has already killed a whole family in the neighborhood, last night."

I can travel beyond the world that I live in, that's the reason I can see my father still. But I will say that the journey isn't that gracious.

I realized some force was trying to pull me to my past, maybe the girl who was coming to meet me was me from the past. I was beginning to put together some sense to all the things that have been happening since morning.

The forest, a labyrinth of shadows, closed in around me. A cold dread settled in my bones as the unseen pursuer's footsteps grew louder, their relentless pursuit echoing through the dense undergrowth. I was a child again, lost and terrified, my heart pounding against my ribs. A faint voice, barely audible above the rustling leaves, urged me forward. A woman, her silhouette barely visible in the dim light, beckoned me with outstretched arms, offering a glimmer of hope in the terrifying darkness.

"Do you see something Aza?", Viansh shook my hand as he kept asking me what's going on.

"Let's meet tonight, call Ekaksh. I need to go now", I responded.

I took my scooter, and asked my friend, Razia, to take my remaining classes for the day.

My father whispered, "go to the lady in black."

I had to venture to the world that falls between the spirit and evil's realm to find my answers. I had to convince all six of them to participate in a planchette.*

I reached home and knocked on Abhaya's room, she was listening to a podcast, I asked her to help me out, even though reluctant, she agreed to help me for the last time (that happens to be every time). By late evening, Shloka, Abhaya, Ekaksh, Viansh, Asmi, Arit and I gathered around Abhaya's planchette board. We started the ceremony and Abhaya's room was pitch dark, with candles around the board.

Suddenly, we heard one of the corridor windows slamming back and forth. Abhaya asked us to concentrate on the planchette call, we had to be able to call Daksh's mom, Diksha, who left us recently, to ask her for some answers as advised by my dad.

From the corridor, I can see the woman with bangles, standing and staring at all of us. She had blood dripping all over the place. Shloka was nervously trembling with her eyes closed. I tried to ignore the woman, but in a split second, she was right next to me.

She was trying to get hold of Shloka, just then Abhaya chanted a hymn loudly and pushed me into the spirit realm. I grabbed her hand and pulled her in with me. She started to bite my hand. I screamed loudly. My dad came to the rescue, he took her by the neck and ripped her into pieces.

---

* *Planchette is an ancient practice to summon the spirits you know to help get answers.*

Wounded and bleeding, I entered Diksha's wooden cabin on the edge of the forest. People used to call her "The Old Witch". For me, she was my grandmother and an old friend of my mom's.

The door swung open, unleashing a torrent of darkness. A deafening chorus of leathery wings filled the air as a swarm of human-bat hybrids, remnants of Viansh's past, descended upon me. Their claws raked across my flesh, leaving me reeling, my vision blurred by a crimson haze. I was a trapped prey, a helpless victim in the clutches of a living nightmare.

In the darkest corner of the room, I can see an oil lit lamp, and a woman sitting and reading a book. That's her! I hurried to her, but as I came closer, the woman had started to break into tiny pieces. They were all the raven witches from Abhaya's past.

The fire from the lamp had turned into a larger flame. The raven witches had started to pounce on dead corpses, amidst which there were kids, dogs, men and women. The air had started to smell pungent, and I was starting to get sick. I got hold of a witch staff and started to hit them, as I needed to cross this chaos sooner as Abhaya's planchette call was starting to fade.

Just then a door opened from another room and Diksha took me into a dark closet.

"My child, run as you have been cursed", she whispered, "but first you need to save the kids of "Shikaar Nagar" from the deadly maneater at prowl. You have fought and won from it before."

I said, "but how?"

In my head, I knew there was some connection between me, the little girl and her mom.

"How do I get rid of it?", I asked.

"By facing your fear!", exclaimed Diksha as she vanished.

A cat from an old coat in the closet appeared, I could remember his eyes from Ekaksh's school hallway.

A voice whispered, as the cat walked to the window of the closet, showing me the direction to leave. "The last time it attacked your mom, you gave in to your fear and let her die. This time don't let it win."

We all were back in the room, and I opened my eyes. Ekaksh asked me to start quickly, saying "looks like there has been another ambush on a family, and the maneater has taken their only daughter."

I could see where it was taking it.

I asked him to follow me in his jeep, towards the cave at the tail end of the forest.

I entered the past again...

The mother's voice, a trembling whisper, drifted up to the terrified girl perched high in the tree. "Rest now, child," she urged, her eyes filled with a mixture of fear and determination. The little girl, her heart pounding in her chest, obeyed, her body going limp as sleep overtook her. Below, the mother stood as a lone sentinel, her courage a flickering flame against the encroaching darkness of the man-eater. The beast had clamped its jaws onto the woman's arm, tearing away half of her flesh, exposing her bone. The mother's strength was waning, her body beginning to give way under the creature's relentless assault. Her screams echoed through the forest, a chilling cry for help that seemed to pierce the very heart of the darkness. The man-eater, emboldened by its victim's weakening resistance, tightened its grip, its eyes glinting with a savage hunger. The little girl, stirred from her slumber by her mother's cries, peered down from her hiding place, her heart filled with terror. She watched helplessly as the beast continued its merciless attack, her mother's screams growing weaker with each passing moment.

"Wake up AzaGka!" I heard my father in my ears.

The sun had long dipped below the horizon, casting the forest in an eerie, twilight gloom. Even in the brightest of days, this part of the woods was shrouded in perpetual darkness. My heart pounded in my chest as I sensed a presence behind us, a shadow moving through the dense undergrowth. I knew it was him, my father, but fear paralyzed me, preventing me from turning to face the inevitable.

"Hurry!" said Ekaksh.

The cave's mouth yawned before us; I was trapped in a dark, menacing portal of the "evil realm". As I ventured deeper into its depths, I felt a chill run down my spine, a premonition of the horrors that awaited. The air was thick with the stench of decay, and the flickering torchlight revealed a gruesome scene. A man, his eyes bloodshot and crazed, was feasting on the lifeless body of a raccoon. He was the demon from Ram's bachelorhood, a creature of pure evil. His gaze, cold and predatory, locked onto mine.

As I readied myself for battle, a pair of icy hands gripped my arm. It was Tiksha, Daksh's wife. Her skin was pale and clammy, her hands stained with dried blood. A shiver ran down my spine as I hesitated, unsure whether her touch would offer protection or lead me into further danger.

The demon's claws raked across my flesh, leaving deep, bleeding wounds. I fought back with a feral fury, my movements hindered by Tiksha's icy grip. Desperation gnawed at me as I realized I was alone, a solitary soul facing an unyielding darkness. Yet, a strange energy surged through me, a primal force that defied exhaustion. Tiksha's hands, cold and clammy, seemed to channel this newfound strength. I was no longer a human, but a beast unleashed, a creature of pure rage.

With a roar that echoed through the cavern, I seized a massive stone and brought it down upon the demon, the impact shattering the silence. The creature howled in pain, its eyes filled with a feral fury. I continued to pummel it, my strength seemingly limitless. The demon, sensing its impending defeat, lashed out with a final, desperate attack, its claws aimed at my throat. But Tiksha, with a swift movement, intercepted the blow, shielding me from harm.

As the demon collapsed, its life force extinguished, I collapsed to the ground, panting heavily. I was alive, victorious, but the cost had been high. My body ached, my mind reeling from the intensity of the battle. Yet, I knew that I had survived, not just for myself, but for Tiksha's sacrifice even after her untimely demise. And I knew somewhere, Ram and Daksh were behind all of this, even though they never played an active role.

I glanced at the maneater from far and could hear the ruthless call of the little girl.

The moment had arrived, my destiny sealed. With a roar that echoed through the forest, I transformed, my human form melting away, replaced by a sleek, powerful tiger. My eyes, now blazing emerald-green, scanned the surrounding undergrowth, searching for my prey. My heart pounded in my chest, a primal rhythm driving me forward.

With a speed that defied belief, I launched myself at the man-eater, my claws outstretched, my teeth bared. The creature, taken aback by my sudden transformation, tried to evade my attack, but it was too late. I pounced, sinking my teeth into its flesh, tearing at its throat with a savage ferocity. The man-eater howled in pain, its struggles futile against my overwhelming strength. With a final, guttural roar, I tore into its flesh, devouring it whole.

As the creature's lifeblood drained away, I collapsed to the ground, panting heavily. The transformation had taken its toll, but I had prevailed. The man-eater was dead, its reign of terror finally ended.

Ekaksh, his face etched with grief, carried the little girl away from the scene. The child, her eyes filled with tears, watched helplessly as her mother's lifeless body lay sprawled on the forest floor. I was that little girl once, powerless to save her mother, trapped by fear. But now, I had become the protector, the avenger. The man-eater was no more, and I had finally found the courage I had lacked so long ago.

Ekanksh and I reached home, we parked at the garage, smiled at each other and headed inside.

"Viansh what's for dinner tonight?", I shouted from the patio.

"I cannot find Shloka, Abhaya and Asmi", shouted Viansh in a troubled tone from inside.

I could see three crows sitting and staring at me from our courtyard. A little girl with no eyes, looking at me from across the road, that's my past, when I was Avannya.

"Looks like I know what the curse is..."

* * * * *

To be continued....

A few short stories, from my "2minhorrorstories" collection. Don't forget to visit: "https://www.justutter.com".

EYES

We had recently moved to a new house in Kali Gali. Our landlord had advised us to avoid one particular room, which we used as a storage room for extra groceries and old furniture. One afternoon, feeling unwell, I forgot to lock the room's door. While napping, I awoke to the shocking sight of an old woman sitting at the edge of my cot, staring at me.

I remained motionless, trying to stay calm. Despite my fear, I managed to close my eyes and suppress a scream. I felt a wave of nausea and peed myself. It was as if darkness was penetrating my soul, and my body was trembling uncontrollably. Luckily, the doorbell rang, saving me from the terrifying encounter.

My neighbor had come to ask for sugar. Distraction provided a brief respite as the woman vanished. I rushed out of the room and locked the door behind me.

That night, my husband and I left for a tour, leaving our helper in charge for a few days. Unfortunately, I had forgotten to mention the haunted room or the woman. When we returned, our helper was terrified. He told us that the woman had stared at him while he slept and had even grabbed his hand, leaving burn marks. The old woman had apparently been burned to death by her son, who had ignored her cries for help.

SOMEONE IS OUT THERE

As children, my cousins and I would spend our summers at my grandparents' house in Bhitarkanika, Odisha. One afternoon, we were playing hide-and-seek in the nearby mangrove forests. I was always the first to be found, so I decided to find a better hiding spot.

I ventured deeper into the forest, climbing a large tree with thick branches. From my perch, I noticed a slightly older girl sitting in the highest branches, dangling her feet. Her silver anklets jingled as she swayed back and forth.

Suddenly, I felt a tug on my ponytail. "Who's there?" I asked, turning to see the girl. She was wearing a green frock and had silver anklets. She giggled and introduced herself, offering to show me a better hiding spot.

As we walked through the forest, I noticed that my cousins were nowhere to be found. It was getting late, and it was her turn to hide. Suddenly, I saw one of her anklets lying near a disturbing sight: a skeleton surrounded by bones, dried blood, and clumps of hair. I felt nauseous and called out for her, but she was nowhere to be seen.

I looked up and saw a shadow watching me from the top of the tree where she had been sitting. It resembled an animal, squatting and hooting like an owl. I ran as fast as I could, following a green frock in the distance.

Eventually, I reached my grandparents' house, covered in dirt and sweat. My cousins were worried about me, as I had ventured into a part of the forest where unexplained deaths and disappearances had occurred years ago. A disturbed killer had been caught and killed after kidnapping and murdering several children.

I tried to find the girl with the green frock but eventually gave up. Then, I stumbled upon an old, torn poster of a missing girl near the market street. It sent chills down my spine. I learned that she had been missing for over ten years. It was impossible for her to be alive and playing hide-and-seek in the forest. Did she help and save me, even though she had been tragically killed herself?

* * * * *

THE CHAIR OUTSIDE THE WINDOW

My family moved to a house near a small town on the outskirts of the city. As a government doctor, my father had the house assigned to us, and fortunately, it was always clean and furnished. My brother and I, being kids, eagerly explored the spacious house and backyard.

One night, as I gazed out my window, I noticed an old, dusty chair on the patio. It looked like an antique piece. Feeling thirsty, I got up to get some water and was startled to see someone sitting on the chair. Exhausted, I dismissed it as a dream and went back to sleep.

The next day, I asked my father if any of his colleagues or patients had visited late last night. He said he had fallen asleep early. That night, I asked my brother to sleep with me, but he was fast asleep. To my dismay, I saw someone sitting on the chair again. Gathering my courage, I approached the window and hid behind the curtains.

It was dark outside, and fog had settled over our patio. The person remained motionless, sitting on the chair. I cautiously opened the door, clutching a cricket bat. The cold air and fog enveloped me, but I could still see the figure sitting on the chair. I screamed and switched on the lights. To my astonishment, there was no one there. However, I noticed fresh mud around the chair, as if someone had been sitting on it with muddy shoes. The next day, an old man visited and insisted on taking the chair away. He explained that it belonged to the previous homeowner, who had recently died in a car accident.

"No Fear,

No Tear,

Only Spear,

To Make Your Steer

Come Closer To You..."